Ashley's Elephant

written by Evan Zaretsky

illustrated by Barbara Spurll

Ashley was a curious little girl who loved her pets. She had a dog. She had a cat. She had a fish. She had a bird. There was even a fox in the neighborhood that she claimed as her own. But all that wasn't enough for Ashley. Oh no. She wanted more!

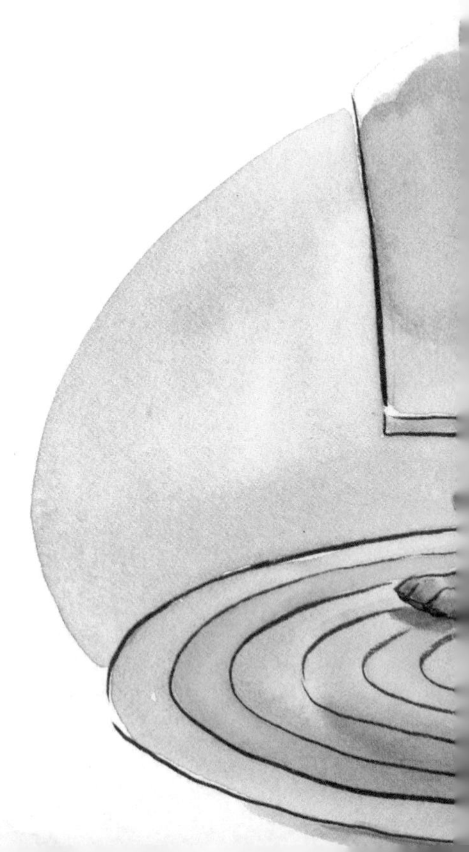

One day Ashley went to her mom and said, "Mom, I have a dog. I have a cat. I have a fish. I have a bird. I even have a fox. But, what I really want is an elephant."

"An elephant!" her mom shouted. "Do you know what to do with a pet elephant, Ashley?"

"Yes!" answered Ashley.

"Do you know what an elephant eats?"

"Yes!" answered Ashley.

"Do you know where to keep a pet elephant?”

“Yes…no,” answered Ashley.

“Then you can’t have a pet elephant,” her mom said.

So Ashley went to think about where she could keep her pet elephant. She thought for one day. She thought for two days. She thought for three days. Ashley spent a whole week thinking. When she was finished thinking she called her friend Jordan.

"Meet me at the pond in five minutes, Jordan. I have an idea."

"Uh oh," said Jordan. A few minutes later Jordan met Ashley at the pond.

"What's your idea this time, Ashley?" Jordan asked his grinning friend.

"Well, I have a dog, a cat, a fish, and a bird. I even have a fox. But, what I really want is an elephant!"

"An elephant!" Jordan shouted. "Ashley, do you know how to wash a pet elephant?"

"Yes!" answered Ashley.

"Do you know where to keep a pet elephant?"

"Yes!" answered Ashley.

"Do you know how to clean up after a pet elephant?"

"Yes...no," answered Ashley.

"Then you can't have a pet elephant," Jordan said.

"Well, I want one. An elephant would make a great pet for me," Ashley stated.

"Where would you keep this elephant?" asked Jordan.

"Well, I thought about that. I can't keep it in my room. I can't keep it in my closet. I can't keep it under my bed. I can't keep it in my basement. I can't keep it in my backyard, my kitchen, or even my bathroom," said Ashley.

"You've already spent a long time thinking about this," said Jordan.

"Yes, I have, and I decided that I will keep my pet elephant here at the pond," answered Ashley.

“The pond! You can’t keep an elephant at the pond. The pond is for turtles, fish, ducks, geese, and sometimes a noisy seagull. The pond is not for elephants,” stated Jordan.

“Well, it is now!” Ashley proclaimed.

That evening Ashley told her mom and dad about her plan.

"I have decided that I will keep my pet elephant at the pond," said Ashley.

"The pond!" her dad shouted.

"You can't keep an elephant at the pond. The pond is for turtles, fish, ducks, geese, and sometimes a noisy seagull. The pond is not for elephants," said her mom.

"Well, it is now!" Ashley insisted. "The pond is the perfect place for my elephant."

"Ashley, do you know what to feed an elephant?" asked her dad.

"Yes!" answered Ashley.

"Do you know how to walk an elephant?" asked her mom.

"Yes!" answered Ashley.

"Do you know how to care for an elephant?" asked her dad.

"Yes...sort of," answered Ashley.

"We'll make you a deal," her mom and dad told her. "If you can take care of your dog, your cat, your fish, your bird, and the neighborhood fox, all by yourself, for one month, then you can have a pet elephant."

"It's a deal," said Ashley, and she walked away pleased with herself.

"She can't care for all those animals," said her dad.

"She'll never be able to do it," agreed her mom.

"Yes, I will!" called Ashley from the next room.

The very next day Ashley began training and caring for all of her pets. A week passed and she was off to a great start. Ashley had no trouble taking care of her dog, her cat, her bird, and her fish all by herself. The fox was nowhere to be seen.

By the end of the second week, the dog learned to roll over. The cat slept quietly by Ashley's side. The bird chirped each morning and the fish continued swimming in his clean bowl. Ashley left peanut butter and jelly sandwiches for the fox.

After three weeks, the dog brought Ashley her slippers. The cat cleaned her own litter box. The bird took the place of Ashley's alarm clock and the fish continued swimming in his clean bowl. The fox ate peanut butter and jelly sandwiches out of Ashley's hand.

At the end of the month, the dog was eating at the kitchen table. The cat was cleaning her hairs off the couch. The bird was baking muffins for Ashley. The fish continued to swim in his clean bowl while the fox brought in the morning newspaper for Ashley's family.

Ashley's mom and dad were amazed that she was able to care for all of her animals and still do all of her school work at the same time. They still didn't believe that she could take care of an elephant, but they had made a promise, and a promise is a promise.

So one afternoon, when Ashley came home from school, there was an enormous, grey, wrinkly elephant standing on the sidewalk.

Ashley called Jordan right away.

“Jordan, I got my elephant! I got my elephant!” she shouted into the phone.

“Uh-oh,” answered Jordan. He rushed to Ashley’s house.

“She’s huge. If we ride on her back we can be anywhere we want in just three steps!” Jordan exclaimed.

"See, I knew you'd like my elephant. Now let's get her to the pond," said Ashley.

They both climbed up onto the elephant's back and went tramping off down the street.

When they got to the pond the elephant was hungry. She was looking for something to eat. She took her long, grey trunk, picked up a tree and swallowed it whole. She munched on bushes for a snack and, to wash it all down, she dipped her trunk into the pond and drank all of the water. When she was done, the green pond looked more like a brown desert.

“Don’t worry. I have another idea,” said Ashley.

“Uh-oh,” said Jordan.

Ashley and Jordan rode the elephant to the zoo. They set her out in the field where she could drink all the water she wanted, eat all the trees she could, and munch on bushes until she was full.

"Thank you, thank you!" said the zookeeper. "We only have one elephant and he has been very lonely. He'll be so excited to have a new friend to play with."

"I'm just glad she's happy," smiled Ashley, as she and Jordan started their long walk home.

"So, have you learned your lesson?" asked Jordan.

"What's that?" asked Ashley.

"That even if you want a pet elephant and can have a pet elephant, you probably shouldn't," said Jordan.

"You're right, Jordan. I still want a pet elephant, and I can have a pet elephant, but I probably shouldn't have one. But, do you know what else I have always really wanted?" asked Ashley.

"Uh-oh," winced Jordan.

ZOO

Ashley grinned from ear to ear. "I have always really wanted a hippopotamus!" exclaimed Ashley.